To the Dragon Master Reading This Book,

I am Griffith, the royal wizard to King Roland the Bold. I train the Dragon Masters who live in his castle.

Over the years, I have learned many things about Dragon Masters and dragons. I have studied magical creatures and fantastic places around the world. I also know secrets about many important wizards. I thought it was a good idea to put all of this knowledge into a book.

I may be a great wizard, but I am not a great writer. I turned to my friend Tracey of the West for help with this project. She is a teller of tales, and she agreed to turn my notes into a guidebook. Some of my other friends have contributed to this book, too.

Read on! Soon you will become the best Dragon Master you can hope to be!

Yours in magic,

Griffith of the Green Fields

GRIFFITH OF THE GREEN FIELDS

MAGIC LEVEL

47 Nobody is sure what the highest magic level is. Magnus of the High Mountains says he can do Level 100 spells, but nobody has ever seen him do one.

COLOR OF MAGIC

POWERS

Griffith is best at magical spells that use potions or rhymes. He can also perform magic simply by pointing his finger. He can transform things, move things, and make force fields.

Griffith grew up in the land of Greenshire, and his parents were farmers. Griffith learned he was a wizard at the age of five. He pointed at a bowl of mushy porridge and transformed it into an apple cake, and his terrified parents sent him to live at the Castle of the Wizards in Belerion. He studied and grew up there.

At eighteen, Griffith found a position as the royal wizard for King Harold of Bracken. For many years, he performed simple tricks to amuse the king and his guests. Then Harold's grandson, King Roland, took the throne. That is when Griffith began to study dragons.

The Castle of the Wizards

Belerion means "Land's End" in the ancient language of the land of Albion. Ages ago, the first wizards gathered in Belerion. Over time, a castle was built, and it became a place of learning. When a child shows signs of being magical, he or she is brought here.

Every wizard takes a name from the land of their birth. I am named for the green fields of my homeland.

-Griffith

GRIFFITH'S WORKSHOP

A workshop is a place to think, to learn, and to create magic spells and potions. Griffith's workshop is on the bottom level of King Roland's castle.

Hairs of a Unicorn Mane

Unicorns will only give them to you if you ask nicely.

UNICORN HAIRS

Treasury of Dragons Around the World

When young King Roland took the throne, he gave Griffith this important book. He commanded Griffith to learn everything there was to learn about dragons. That is when Griffith's love of dragons began.

Griffith uses herbs to make all sorts of potions. He gets many of the herbs from Bracken. His wizard friends send him some, too.

Out of Sight

Three drops of this will turn you invisible for one hour.

Condor Feathers

Perfect for flight potions.

Here is lavender from my garden!
—D

Moonbeams

These can strengthen spells, but they are difficult to catch.

Wizard

DIEGO OF THE
SANDY SHORES

MAGIC LEVEL
51

COLOR OF MAGIC

POWERS

Diego has the power to transport himself anywhere in the world by snapping his fingers. He is a very good potion maker. Diego also has the magical ability to communicate with animals.

Flying Friend

One of Diego's animal friends is Bob, a seagull. He helps out when Diego asks him to.

Diego was born in the Land of Aragon. He attended the Castle of the Wizards, where he and Griffith became good friends. Then, when he was twelve, he was chosen to assist a wizard named Leda of the Raging River.

Leda had discovered a nest of baby Fire Dragons in the land of Allaben. There were too many for her to care for on her own. So she and Diego studied them together. Diego went on to become an expert in baby dragons.

Diego's Cottage

Today, Diego lives in a cottage by the ocean in the Land of Aragon. He trains Carlos, the Dragon Master of a baby Lightning Dragon named Lalo.

A Magical Alarm

The seashells hanging from the wall of Diego's cottage rattle when danger is near.

Wizard
HULDA OF THE
ICY PLAINS

MAGIC LEVEL

53

COLOR OF MAGIC

POWERS

Hulda is an expert in magic words, spells, and charms. When you say a spell to give an object magical powers, that object becomes charmed.

Charmed Object

Hulda charmed this spoon for the castle cook so that anything the cook makes with it will taste delicious!

BACKGROUND

Hulda comes from a long line of wizards in the Far North Lands who are sent to Belerion to train. Hulda studied at the Castle of the Wizards with Griffith and Diego. Wizards from the Far North return home to serve their king or queen when they turn eighteen.

The rulers in the Far North always keep Ice Dragons, and the wizards there have been training Dragon Masters to work with these dragons for hundreds of years.

Hulda trains Mina, the Dragon Master of an Ice Dragon named Frost.

Hulda's Lost Sister

Hulda's sister Astrid is the only wizard with dark magic strong enough to equal Maldred's. Years ago, Astrid and Maldred got into a great magical battle. Astrid has not been seen since, but Hulda believes that her sister is alive.

If Astrid does return, there is sure to be trouble.

MAGICAL OBJECTS AND TOOLS

Magical objects are items that have been charmed by wizards to do magical things. Dragon Masters and others can sometimes use them.

Magic Mirrors

Give one mirror to the person you want to communicate with, and you two can talk through the mirrors no matter how far apart you are. The mirrors can also act as mini portals. You can send a small object through a mirror, and it will come out through the other mirror.

Feathers of Finding

Green swallows live on top of only one mountain in a faraway land across the ocean from Bracken. If you are lucky enough to get one of their feathers, it can be charmed to help you find a lost object. Ask the feather to lead you to the object, and then follow it!

Most wizards can create magic just by pointing a finger. But magical tools are items that wizards often use to help them create magic.

Gazing Balls

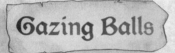

This magical glass ball allows wizards to see what is happening in other places around the world. Some of the most powerful wizards can use them to see the past and the future.

Wands

Every wizard begins learning how to cast spells by using a wand made from an ash tree or oak tree. As their powers get stronger, wizards can cast spells without using wands. However, many wizards continue to use wands to give their spells an extra boost. Some even charm their wands to make them stronger.

KING ROLAND
THE BOLD

King Roland rules the Kingdom of Bracken. He is the son of King Edward, who was the son of King Harold. Roland became king at the age of twenty-two. He began his search for dragons soon after he took the throne.

King Roland is loud and gets angry easily. But he has a good heart. And marrying Queen Rose helped to bring out more of his good side.

Look for more about King Roland's quest for dragons later in this book.

-Griffith

QUEEN ROSE
THE JUST

Queen Rose treats people fairly, which is why she is called Queen Rose the Just. She is also kind and intelligent.

The queen ruled the Kingdom of Arkwood on her own before she married King Roland. Now they rule the two kingdoms — Bracken and Arkwood — together. Queen Rose's subjects were happy that she didn't move to a faraway kingdom.

Queen Rose is very interested in the well-being of the dragons. She encourages King Roland to take good care of them.

THE KINGDOM OF BRACKEN

Bracken is one kingdom in the larger land known as Albion.

Old Oak Woods

Farmers' Village

Farming Fields

Market Square

KING ROLAND'S CASTLE

King Harold used the underground floor of the castle as a dungeon, but King Roland turned it into a place where Dragon Masters can work with their dragons.

THE DRAGON UNDERCROFT

Classroom

This is where Dragon Masters learn their lessons. It holds bookshelves filled with books about dragons.

Training Room

This is where King Roland's Dragon Masters begin their training. The dragons can practice using their powers on command in this safe, indoor space.

Griffith's Workshop

This room contains potions, herbs, and other items used for spells. Griffith's Dragon Stone is here, as well as other magical objects and tools.

Dragon Caves

Comfortable spaces for the dragons to sleep and eat.

Tunnel to Valley of Clouds

This tunnel leads to a hidden valley surrounded by hills. The valley is the perfect spot for flying practice because the dragons can fly without anyone seeing them.

KING ROLAND'S QUEST
FOR DRAGONS

When King Roland was fourteen years old, Bracken
was attacked by the Kingdom of Dunkelberg. He bravely
joined the battle, fighting alongside his father to protect
Bracken. His grandfather died during that battle, but
Roland fought on and Bracken won. That is how he
earned the name Roland the Bold.

Eight years later, Roland's father died peacefully, and
Roland became king. From that day on, Roland decided
to make Bracken the most protected place on Earth.
He believed that one thing could protect his kingdom:
dragons. So he asked Griffith to help him learn about
dragons around the world.

The king sent his soldiers out to capture all kinds of dragons. Griffith did not agree with the king's actions. Taking the dragons from their homes seemed cruel. And when the dragons first came to the castle, they were wild and upset. King Roland ordered them to be locked in their caves.

Thanks to the books Griffith had read, he knew that he needed to find Dragon Masters for the dragons right away. But first, he had to find a Dragon Stone!

DRAGON STONES

Dragon Masters and wizards both use Dragon Stones, but in different ways.

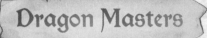

Dragon Masters

Every Dragon Master wears a small piece of the Dragon Stone. At first, the Dragon Master can give the dragon simple commands. When their bond grows strong, and they can reach each other's minds, the stone will glow green. This connection becomes even stronger as the Dragon Master and dragon work together.

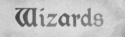

Wizards

If a wizard wants to train a Dragon Master, he or she must first find a Dragon Stone. Wizards cannot communicate with dragons. But they can ask their Dragon Stone to choose a Dragon Master to match with a dragon. An image of the Dragon Master will appear inside a green beam of light given off by the stone.

The Secret of Green Lake

Getting my Dragon Stone was not easy. I knew that wizards in the Far North Lands had been using these stones for many years. So I asked my wizard friend Hulda where to find one. She told me that a piece of the prime stone might be found in the bottom of a magical body of water known as Green Lake.

I traveled far to reach the lake. Once I got there, I dove to the very bottom. I found my Dragon Stone and brought it back to Bracken. Then I used it to find Dragon Masters for King Roland's dragons.

-Griffith

THE PRIME STONE

Every Dragon Stone in the world comes from one very big, very old stone: the prime stone. It is hidden inside the Pyramid of the Seven Dragons, in the Land of Pyramids.

Every ten thousand years, energy from the prime stone creates a Lightning Dragon egg. The stone feeds energy to the egg, so its powers are weakened until the egg hatches.

Nobody is sure how old the prime stone is, or where it came from. Is it a wonder of nature? Was it created by powerful wizards, or some other kind of magic? There may be more secrets to be discovered inside that pyramid.

A HISTORY OF DRAGON MASTERS

These four Dragon Masters are some of the most famous in history.

Ancient scrolls say that the first Dragon Master was Ast, from the Land of Pyramids. She was chosen by the prime Dragon Stone more than two thousand years ago.

Ast

Justina

Five hundred years later, a Dragon Master named Justina from Byzantia fought for the safety of dragons. She rescued and took care of dragons that had been captured and mistreated.

Blind since birth, this Dragon Master is remembered for his beautiful poetry about dragons. He lived one thousand years ago in the Land of the Far East.

Jia

Borg

This young Dragon Master is famous in tales from the Land of the Far North. Six hundred years ago, Borg and his Ice Dragon, Halvor, defended their village from an attack by sea. Halvor froze the water with his icy breath!

Rules of the Stone

- The Dragon Stone almost always chooses a Dragon Master who is eight years old. Some experts think this might be the best age for a human and dragon to make a connection. The hearts and minds of children this age are open to new ideas.

- A Dragon Master will always keep the connection to their dragon. But if a Dragon Master needs to give up that connection for any reason, a new Dragon Master can be chosen.

Dragon Masters come from all over the world, and they are all different. Not all can see, or hear, or walk. But all Dragon Masters have good hearts.

–Griffith

How to Care for Your Dragon

Depending upon the type of dragon you have, your dragon might need special care. But every dragon needs three basic things: food, shelter, and a good scale scrubbing now and then.

Feeding Your Dragon

Earth Dragons prefer food that grows in the ground, like carrots or potatoes. Fire Dragons love spicy food, like peppers. Water Dragons love to eat fish. Your dragon will let you know his or her favorite food when you connect.

Dragons do not need to eat every day. But after they use their powers, they are extra hungry!

Your Dragon's Nest

Most dragons like to have their own area to sleep and rest. Make sure that your dragon has a room or a space big enough for them to move around in. Add plenty of fresh hay to make a nice soft bed.

Shining Dragon Scales

Not every dragon's scales are shiny, but dragons all like to have their scales brushed and cleaned.

 Dragon Master
DRAKE GEORGE

HOME

Drake was born in the Kingdom of Bracken. He lives there still, now in King Roland's castle.

Drake's Silver Sword

This special sword was a gift from Jean Arcand, the Dragon Master of the Silver Dragon. Drake can use it to create portals that allow him to travel between far-apart places. The more he uses the sword, the more he may discover about its powers.

STRENGTHS

Drake is friendly and eager to learn new things. He will always do what is needed to save the day. When he first came to the castle, he didn't feel like he belonged. But thanks to his friendship with Bo, and connection to Worm, he gained confidence.

Drake comes from a family of expert onion growers in Bracken's Farmers' Village. He worked in the fields with his mother, Matilda, and his five older brothers: Arthur, Byron, Clinton, Darren, and Kelvin.

DRAGON

Worm the Earth Dragon

THE FARMERS' VILLAGE

Most people who live in the Kingdom of Bracken are farmers. Family members work together to grow vegetables: oats, barley, beans, peas, wheat, potatoes, cabbages, parsnips, carrots, spinach, or onions.

peas

potatoes

barley

onions

oats

Each family gives part of the harvest to King Roland to feed the residents of the castle. The farmers are free to eat, trade, or sell the rest in the market.

cabbages

carrots

wheat

beans

parsnips

spinach

Dragon
WORM THE
EARTH DRAGON

Worm is an amazing dragon.
The powers of his mind can do almost
anything!

DRAGON MASTER

Drake George

POWERS

- Worm can instantly transport to any place in the world.

- He can move things using the power of his mind. He can make objects float and fly, or even throw them. He can break apart rocks and walls.

  - He can use his energy to create a protective shield.

  - He can often sense when danger is coming.

  - He can shoot beams from his eyes.

POWER COLOR

SIZE

LENGTH: 42 feet

WEIGHT: 7,100 pounds

Training Tip

Feeding Worm apples will put him in a good mood before a training session.

EARTH DRAGONS

Earth Dragons live deep underground in tunnels and very rarely come to the surface. While most other dragons live alone, Earth Dragons prefer to live together. Explorers have found as many as twelve in one place.

All Earth Dragons have very strong mind powers. Why, then, do they live hidden away? No one knows for sure. But it may be because they are peaceful creatures who simply enjoy one another's company.

Some dragon experts believe that Earth Dragons are related to the Naga, a legendary Earthquake Dragon. Earth Dragons and the Naga have similar powers. Earth Dragons can move things with their minds. The Naga can make the earth shake just by thinking about it.

The Naga

I also wonder if Earth Dragons are related to the Time Dragon in Casgore. Earth Dragons can transport to any place. Time Dragons can transport to any place and time.

-Griffith

◆ Dragon Master
RORI SMITH

⟨ HOME ⟩

Rori was born in the Kingdom of Bracken. She lives there still, now in King Roland's castle.

⟨ STRENGTHS ⟩

Rori is very brave, and she is a good problem solver. She is not afraid to fight for what she believes in. She has a strong will, which sometimes means she doesn't like to follow orders. And while she likes to argue with people, she never argues with her best friend, Ana.

Key to the Castle

The key Rori swiped from one of the castle guards isn't magic, but it is pretty close. She can use it to open any lock in the castle.

BACKGROUND

Before becoming a Dragon Master, Rori lived with her mother, Dorothy, her father, William, and her two sisters, Grace and Emma. William is a blacksmith.

DRAGON

Vulcan the Fire Dragon

THE CRAFTERS' VILLAGE

All of the makers in the Kingdom of Bracken live and work in this village. Rori's family lives here.

Carpenter's Shop

If you need a chair or a table, this is where to go.

Bows and Arrows

These weapons can be used for hunting—or for defending the kingdom.

This is where I bought the carved box that holds the Dragon Stone.

—Griffith

Tailor's Shop

The workers in this shop make fine clothes.

Bakery

The baker provides the castle with one hundred loaves of bread every morning. Villagers can buy bread here or use the ovens to bake their own bread for a penny.

Blacksmith's Shop

William Smith, Rori's father, works here. He makes tools for farming, and his horseshoes are excellent.

Bucket Shop

Wooden buckets are the best—and only—way to carry water from a well.

Dragon
VULCAN THE FIRE DRAGON

Vulcan's fire blasts are very powerful, but he sometimes has a hard time controlling them.

DRAGON MASTER

Rori Smith

POWERS

- Vulcan can shoot fireballs from his mouth.

- He can shoot streams of fire from his nose.

- He can fly.

POWER COLOR

When Vulcan is happy, he will sometimes shoot sparks out of his nose! But don't get too close to him when he does this. I once lost my beard after Rori told him a joke!

-Griffith

SIZE

LENGTH: 20 feet

WEIGHT: 6,800 pounds

Training Tip

Target practice is very helpful for Vulcan to learn how to control his powers. But it's always good to have a Water Dragon nearby!

FIRE DRAGONS

Fire Dragons are found all over the Middle Lands. There are tales of them from Albion, Gallia, Casgore, Jura, and Remus. Fire Dragons live alone in caves.

People fear Fire Dragons, because their fire powers can be so destructive. But when paired with a Dragon Master, a Fire Dragon can be quite useful.

There is still much to be learned about how to control a Fire Dragon's wild powers. A wizard named Shula is trying to find out where their power comes from. She believes that Fire Dragons may have an inner chamber of fuel inside their bellies.

I have read about Lava Dragons that live in volcanoes. I suspect they may have similar powers to Fire Dragons. It would be exciting to see one in person.

-Griffith

Dragon Master
BO YIN

Bo grew up in the kingdom of Emperor Song. He currently lives at King Roland's castle in the Kingdom of Bracken.

Bo's Silver Shield

Jean Arcand, the Dragon Master of the Silver Dragon, gave Bo this special shield. It is much stronger than an ordinary shield.

STRENGTHS

Bo stays calm when things go wrong. He is sensitive to the feelings of others and was very kind to Drake when Drake first came to Bracken Castle.

BACKGROUND

Back home, Bo lived with his mother and father, Renshu and Fan. He has two younger sisters, Dandan and Jun, and two younger brothers, Heng and Li.

DRAGON

Shu the Water Dragon

EMPEROR SONG

Emperor Song rules a large kingdom in the Land of the Far East. The emperor is fond of dragons. Images of dragons decorate his palace.

He is a fair ruler who allowed Bo to leave the kingdom and go to Bracken at King Roland's request.

The Kingdom of Caves

This kingdom is known for its talented artists and musicians. In the royal city, you will find many sculptures and paintings of dragons.

The Raven Guard

A group of skilled fighters that serves the emperor. They dress all in black and can move silently without being seen. They are excellent spies.

Dragon
SHU THE
WATER DRAGON

Shu's water powers can
have the strength of a
tidal wave. But she has
a gentle spirit.

DRAGON MASTER

Bo Yin

POWERS

- Shu can fly by floating on air currents (just like a boat floats on ocean waves).

- She can shoot streams of water from her mouth.

- She can create great waves using nearby bodies of water.

- She can breathe out a blue mist that can wash away any spell.

POWER COLOR

SIZE

LENGTH: 17 feet

WEIGHT: 2,900 pounds

Training Tip

Shu practices controlling her water powers by aiming blasts at targets.

WATER DRAGONS

Water Dragons can be found in any part of the world where there is water. However, they don't always live *in* water.

In the Land of the Far East, Water Dragons like Shu live in caves near lakes, ponds, and rivers.

Water Dragons have many powers: water powers, the power of flight, and special healing powers.

Sea Dragons and Lake Dragons also have water powers. But they live under the water and never leave it. I have read of one Sea Dragon in the land of Kapua that is very powerful.

-Griffith

Dragon Master

ANA GAMAL

HOME

Ana grew up in the Land of Pyramids. She currently lives at King Roland's castle in the Kingdom of Bracken.

STRENGTHS

Ana has a positive, sunny personality. She is clever and is always figuring out new ways to use her dragon's powers. Ana is a good friend to all of the Dragon Masters who live in the castle.

Ana lost her mother when she was a baby. Her father, Abrax, is a traveling merchant who sells beautiful fabrics. Growing up, Ana went with him on trips to faraway lands. She has seen more places in the world than the other Dragon Masters.

DRAGON

Kepri the Sun Dragon

THE LAND OF PYRAMIDS

This desert land is located south and east of Bracken. It takes thirty days to travel there by horse and boat.

This land rose up on the banks of the River Ar. The great pyramids and temples were built on the riverbanks more than two thousand years ago.

Pyramid of the Seven Dragons

The prime Dragon Stone is hidden deep inside the Pyramid of the Seven Dragons. To reach it, six dragons are needed—and six Dragon Masters with sharp minds!

Dragon Temple

Heru and his family collect and protect secrets of the dragons here.

Today, there are several good schools teaching science there. And because of the river, the Land of Pyramids became a great trading center. Books, fabrics, and spices find their way from this land to places all around the world.

Dragon

KEPRI THE SUN DRAGON

Every Sun Dragon is born with a Moon Dragon twin. Kepri's twin is named Wati.

DRAGON MASTER

Ana Gamal

Training Tip

Ana and Kepri practice making loops in the sky when Kepri flies.

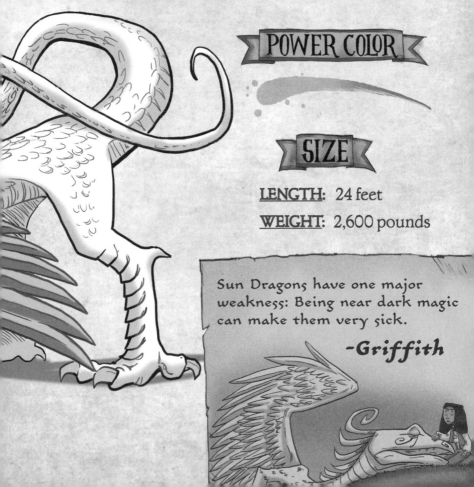

- Kepri is a very graceful, fast flyer.

- Her whole body can light up, just like the sun.

- From her mouth, she can shoot beams of golden sunlight and ribbons of sunlight in different colors.

- She can shoot out balls of light that will hang in the area for a short time.

POWER COLOR

SIZE

LENGTH: 24 feet

WEIGHT: 2,600 pounds

Sun Dragons have one major weakness: Being near dark magic can make them very sick.

-Griffith

Dragon Master
HERU AL-TAREK

HOME

The Land of Pyramids

STRENGTHS

Heru spends most of his time reading ancient books and scrolls about dragons. Soon, he may know more about dragons than any wizard! He and Drake bonded when they searched for the Pyramid of the Seven Dragons together.

Dragon Secrets

Inside the Temple of the Dragons, there is a secret chamber filled with books and scrolls about dragons.

Heru comes from a long line of people who communicate with dragons. (In his land, they do not call these people Dragon Masters.) He lives with his parents, Tarek and Sarah, in the Temple of the Dragons. When he grows up, it will be his job to guard the ancient secrets of the dragons.

DRAGON

Wati the Moon Dragon

Dragon
WATI THE
MOON DRAGON

Wati is very similar to his twin sister, Kepri. But where Kepri is light, Wati is dark.

LENGTH: 24 feet
WEIGHT: 2,600 pounds

Heru al-Tarek

POWERS

- Wati is a very graceful, fast flyer.

- His whole body can glow with dark light, just like the moon.

- From his mouth, he can shoot streams of dark light, and ribbons of moonlight in different colors.

- He can shoot out balls of dark light that hang in the air.

POWER COLOR

Training Tip

Heru always trains Wati in the dark, when it is easiest to see his moon powers at work.

SUN DRAGONS & MOON DRAGONS

by Sarah and Tarek of the Temple of the Dragons

Sun Dragons and Moon Dragons come from the Land of Pyramids. They are always born as twins, from the same egg. The mother dragon can be either a Sun Dragon or a Moon Dragon.

Twin dragons have a special connection. They can communicate with each other over long distances. And they can cure each other of any illness. If the Moon Dragon is sick, the Sun Dragon can cure it with sunlight. If the Sun Dragon is sick, the Moon Dragon can cure it with moonlight.

The powers of each twin are equally strong. But a Sun Dragon's powers are strongest during the day, and a Moon Dragon's powers are strongest at night. They can also combine their powers for an extra-strong strike.

Dragon Master

PETRA MARIS

HOME

Petra grew up in Helas, in the Southern Lands. She currently lives at King Roland's castle in the Kingdom of Bracken.

STRENGTHS

Petra was afraid of being a Dragon Master at first, but she overcame her fears to save Drake and King Roland. She is a good researcher who can find answers to questions quickly. She communicates with a four-headed dragon, which is four times more difficult than communicating with one dragon! Like Heru, she loves to read about dragons. She and Heru write to each other and share notes.

Veggie Master

Petra does not eat meat. Her favorite food from back home is hummus — a spread made of chickpeas, a sesame-seed paste, and garlic.

STRENGTHS

Petra's parents, Daria and Zale, work in the great library in Helas. Her great-great-great-great-uncle Cosmo was a dragon expert. Petra grew up among rows and rows of books from all over the world.

DRAGON

Zera the Poison Dragon

THE SOUTHERN LANDS

The Southern Lands are located southeast of Bracken. Helas, the land where Petra comes from, contains several busy cities. People from all over the world sail to Helas's coasts. Many people stay and live there. They bring their unique customs and food with them.

The Skav Empire

Pliska

Helas

The weather in the Southern Lands is usually much warmer than it is in Bracken. Many delicious vegetables grow there, as well as fruits so bright and colorful, they look like jewels.

Turkland

favorite fruit

Petra loves to eat figs, which grow in warm parts of the world. They are small purple or green fruits with a honey-like taste.

ZERA THE POISON DRAGON

Zera can appear frightening, with her four heads and sizzling poison attacks. But she is a gentle creature with a fascinating hidden power…

Training Tip

When training a four-headed dragon, it is often easier to train one head at a time.

SIZE

LENGTH: 16 feet

WEIGHT: 8,000 pounds

POWER COLOR

- Zera can shoot green poison mist from all four of her mouths. The poison can burn on contact. And it can make humans and other creatures very ill if breathed in.

- Her four heads can sing in perfect harmony. This beautiful song can heal any creature harmed by her poison.

DRAGON MASTER

Petra Maris

I have a feeling that Zera's song may have other powers. It will be interesting to find out if that is true!

-Griffith

POISON DRAGONS

by Petra Maris

Griffith asked me to write about Poison Dragons in his guidebook. He says I know more about them than anybody! I agree with him.

Poison Dragons, also known as Hydras, are very rare. They are found in the Southern Lands, and the last time somebody saw one was one hundred years ago. Zera may be the only one in the world.

No one knows how long a Poison Dragon lives for. I asked Zera how old she was, but even she is not sure. She said she has lived "for a very long time."

Every Poison Dragon has four heads. When I hear Zera's voice inside my head, I hear all four heads talking at once. So I think the four heads all think the same thing at the same time. But I need to spend more time with Zera and read more books to find out for sure.

Warning: Never touch the tail of a Poison Dragon! It makes them nervous. If you need to calm them down, gently pat or scratch one of their heads.

Sound Dragons can make sounds louder and softer. I wonder what a Sound Dragon's powers could do with the song of a Hydra?

-Griffith

CARLOS ALMA

HOME

The Land of Aragon, where he trains with Diego of the Sandy Shores.

STRENGTHS

I invited Carlos to live at the castle in Bracken, but he chose to remain in Aragon to be close to his grandmother.

-Griffith

Carlos took on a big challenge: to train a baby Lightning Dragon that is always shooting sparks! Patience is important when you are training a baby dragon, and Carlos has a lot of it. His grandmother taught him to be helpful and a hard worker.

BACKGROUND

When the Dragon Stone found Carlos, he was living with his grandmother, Nita, in a fishing village.

Abuela

Carlos calls Nita "Abuela," which is the word for grandmother in the old language of Aragon.

DRAGON

Lalo the Lightning Dragon

THE LAND OF ARAGON

Aragon is a large coastal kingdom south of Bracken, and below the land of Gallia. Most of the people there live along the rocky coast. Aragon is known for having great fishermen and women, and skilled boat makers.

Ursa

Sea Inside the Land

Queen Sofia is the ruler of Aragon. Diego of the Sandy Shores is her royal wizard.

Queen Sofia allows Diego to live in his cottage by the sea instead of in the palace. (He can "poof" to the royal city of Ursa quickly if she needs him.)

Dragon
LALO THE
LIGHTNING DRAGON

Lalo is just a baby dragon right now, but his powers are very strong!

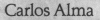
DRAGON MASTER

Carlos Alma

POWERS

- Lalo is made of energy, so he can pass through things that are solid, such as stone walls.

- He can fly with the speed of lightning.

- His wings can create sizzling lightning bolts and sparks.

SIZE

LENGTH: 12 feet

WEIGHT: He will not stay still long enough for Diego to weigh him. And because he is made of energy, it is possible that he doesn't have any real weight.

POWER COLOR

Training Tip

Baby dragons need lots of sleep! Carlos makes sure Lalo is well rested before any training session.

LIGHTNING DRAGONS

Every ten thousand years, energy from the prime Dragon Stone creates an egg. And out of that egg, one Lightning Dragon is born.

There is not much written about Lightning Dragons. Nobody knows how long they live. If the one born ten thousand years ago is still alive, nobody has seen it.

Diego and Carlos are studying Lalo to see what they can learn. They are also trying to figure out if Lightning Dragons and Thunder Dragons are related.

Lightning Dragons do not have parents like other dragons. Lalo was hatched from an energy egg and is the only one of his kind. He appears to be made of energy and does not have a solid body.

Thunder Dragons have parents and solid bodies. For that reason, Diego believes the two types of dragons are not related. (Look for more about Thunder Dragons later in this book.)

-Griffith

BABY DRAGONS
by Diego

My good friend Griffith says I am an expert in baby dragons. I don't know about that! I have helped raise several baby dragons, but there is still so much to learn! Here is what I know . . .

Baby dragons hatch from eggs and are usually raised by their mother and father. They are born with their basic powers, but they do not know how to control them right away. With some dragons — such as Fire Dragons — this can be very dangerous!

In the wild, mother or father dragons keep their babies calm and show them how to use their powers as they grow. A baby dragon without a parent can harm itself or others. In that case, it is helpful to pair the baby dragon with a Dragon Master right away.

When Zera sings, her voice calms Lalo.

-Griffith

When I was a young wizard, I found a nest of three baby Fire Dragons with no parents in sight. It took time to find Dragon Masters for them. In the meantime, I cared for them. I learned that singing to baby dragons helps to calm them. And for the baby Fire Dragons, a splash in a cold pond worked wonders!

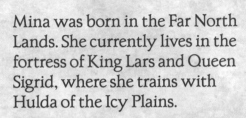

Dragon Master
MINA OF THE FAR NORTH

HOME

Mina was born in the Far North Lands. She currently lives in the fortress of King Lars and Queen Sigrid, where she trains with Hulda of the Icy Plains.

Mina's Ax

Mina's ax might not be magical, but it is very practical. She can use it to chop wood and to break ice when fishing or climbing. She once used it to shatter a magical object to pieces!

STRENGTHS

Like many people of the Far North, Mina is strong in body and spirit. Mina traveled by herself for many days to save her kingdom. She has the true heart of a Dragon Master and she does not give up easily. She formed a bond with King Roland's Dragon Masters and has promised to help them if they ever need it.

BACKGROUND

Mina's parents are Gyda and Erik, animal doctors who began learning how to care for dragons after Mina became a Dragon Master. She has a little brother named Fisk.

DRAGON

Frost the Ice Dragon

THE FAR NORTH LANDS

The Far North Lands are a group of four kingdoms just above Bracken. The kingdoms each have their own rulers.

Hundreds of years ago, the kingdoms were in a long war with one another. Then giants from the Ice Fields attacked the Far North Lands using might and magic. The kingdoms joined together to fight off the giants. There has been peace ever since.

Kingdom of King Lars and Queen Sigrid

Kingdom of Flowers

Frosty Gulf

Kingdom of Queen Eva

In much of these lands, winter lasts for six months out of the year. The people there have learned to live with ice and snow. They spend most of their time outdoors. They even invented a sport that involves pushing a stone across an icy pond with sticks.

Ice Fields

Kingdom
of King Albin

River Joki

Dragon
FROST THE
ICE DRAGON

An Ice Giant named Vasty used magic to turn Frost against Mina and his kingdom. But when Mina broke the spell, Frost helped to save the day!

When Zera the Poison Dragon sprayed poison mist at Frost, he froze all of the droplets in midair before they could harm him.

-Griffith

Mina of the Far North

- Frost has freezing-cold breath.

- He can blast his opponents with an icy chill.

- He can even trap them in a block of ice!

- He is a strong, fast flyer.

SIZE

LENGTH: 20 feet

WEIGHT: 7,800 pounds

Training Tip

Like most Ice Dragons, Frost does not like warm weather. He is happiest training when it is below freezing outside.

POWER COLOR

ICE DRAGONS

Ice Dragons can be found in icy caves all over the Far North Lands. Each kingdom in the Far North Lands keeps an Ice Dragon around for protection.

The neck and belly of each Ice Dragon are covered in fur. This is not because the dragon needs to keep warm. The fur acts as a protective layer to keep the icy air inside the dragon cold.

Ice Dragons can stop all water attacks because they can freeze any water that is aimed at them. If you encounter something that has been frozen by an Ice Dragon, it is not easy to unfreeze it. Fire Dragons have the power needed to melt an Ice Dragon's blasts. There are no Fire Dragons that live in the Far North, so these dragons almost never meet. (Although Vulcan the Fire Dragon and Frost the Ice Dragon did meet once.)

Many dragons have powers that match their habitats. Ice Dragons live in the frozen north. In rocky places, you will find Stone Dragons.

—Griffith

Dragon Master
OBI OKIRO

HOME

Obi lives in the Kingdom of Ifri.

STRENGTHS

Obi is very clever. At first, he thought he was not important enough to be Dayo's Dragon Master. But he has a strong connection to nature and knows about all of the animals in his land. It is his love of animals that helped him connect with Dayo. Obi became friends with Ana and Drake after they came to Ifri to find him.

Obi comes from a farming village where he lives with his mother and father, Bisa and Kasim.

I need to find a wizard in Ifri who can help Obi if he needs it.

-Griffith

DRAGON

Dayo the Rainbow Dragon

THE KINGDOM OF IFRI

The Kingdom of Ifri is a very large land that is south and west of the Land of Pyramids. It contains a desert, a mighty river, a waterfall, and great green fields.

Most people in Ifri live in villages, but there are a few large cities there, too. Several women and men of Ifri are known around the world for their skills in math and medicine. Many people of Ifri are artists who make wonderful sculptures and weave colorful clothing.

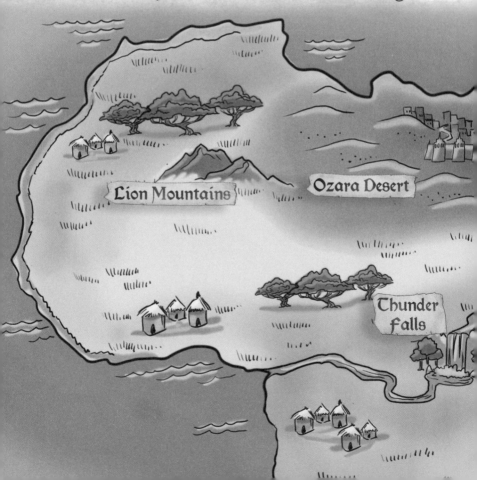

Lion Mountains

Ozara Desert

Thunder Falls

The Marvelous Animals of Ifri

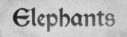

Warthog

This pig-like animal has pointy, curved tusks.

Elephants

These huge beasts are gentle and travel in groups.

Giraffe

This spotted creature has a long neck and eats the leaves of trees.

Apes

These furry animals are very intelligent.

Dragon
DAYO THE
RAINBOW DRAGON

Dayo might be the only dragon who lives in the Kingdom of Ifri. She has a very important power, and she is very, very old.

DRAGON MASTER

Obi Okiro

POWER COLOR

POWERS

- Dayo leaves her cave every spring and brings rain to the land.

- Although Dayo has no wings, she can fly and float in the sky.

- The stripes on Dayo's body are the colors of the rainbow. She looks like a rainbow when she flies across the sky.

SIZE

LENGTH: 48 feet

WEIGHT: 6,800 pounds

Training Tip

Dayo lives in her cave and is so old and powerful that she does not need to be trained by Obi. But they have a very strong connection, and they can call on each other for help at any time.

THE LEGEND OF THE NAGA

From *The Lore of the Ancient One*

This tale begins years ago, when magic was new.

One morning, when the sun came up, the earth began to shake. Trees fell. Mountains crumbled. The ground cracked open.

Then an egg emerged from the deepest part of the earth. It was a huge dragon egg, as big as a mountain.

From that egg, a dragon hatched. This dragon was larger than any dragon that any wizard had ever seen. He was at heart a peaceful dragon, but had no control over his powers. Frightened and wild, he brought down mountains and caused great floods.

The wizards of the north and south needed to save the world from the Naga. They used powerful magic to create two keys: a Silver Key and a Gold Key. These keys gave them control of the Naga and allowed them to send him back to his home deep in the center of the earth. The Silver Key and Gold Key were hidden and are guarded to this day.

The Naga calmed down once safe inside the earth again. And the Dragon Stone also chose a Dragon Master for the Naga to keep watch over him.

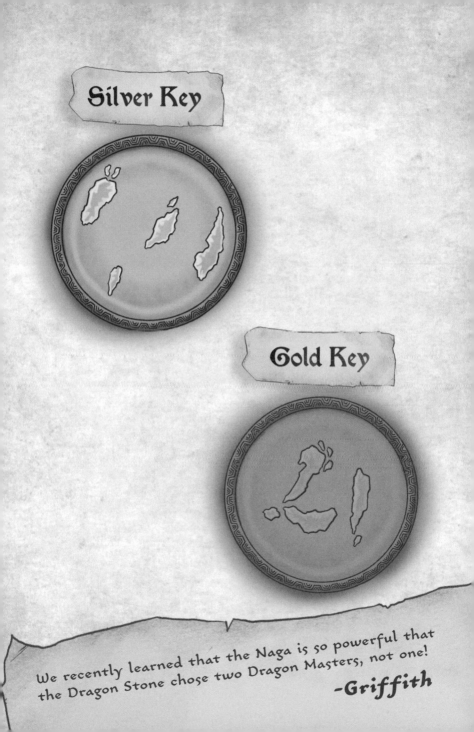

Silver Key

Gold Key

We recently learned that the Naga is so powerful that the Dragon Stone chose two Dragon Masters, not one!

-Griffith

Dragon Master
JEAN ARCAND

HOME

Jean grew up in and still lives in the Land of Gallia.

Jean's Silver Sword

Jean used silver from the Silver Dragon's lair to make this sword, as well as the gifts she gave to Drake and Bo.

DRAGON

Argent the Silver Dragon

STRENGTHS

Jean is a wonderful inventor! She creates tools that she uses to defend her castle, such as catapults. She is the guardian of the Silver Key, and she takes her job very seriously.

Jean's Catapults

A catapult is a device that can launch objects into the air and send them flying very far. Jean's catapults have a heavy weight on one end and a basket of small rocks on the other end. When Jean cuts the rope, the weights drop and the rocks launch into the air.

BACKGROUND

Jean was raised by her mother, Amee, a master sword maker.

THE LAND OF GALLIA

Gallia is a small land not far from Bracken — just a short trip by boat across the Sea of Albion. It has been ruled by King Leon for almost fifty years.

Most of the people of Gallia are farmers. But many live in its largest city, Parisi. That city is known for its great food, poetry, and art.

KING LEON

North Sea

Parisi

Lair of the Silver Dragon

Jean Arcand does not live in the royal castle of Gallia. She lives in a stone castle on a hill in the countryside, far from the royal city. This castle was built hundreds of years ago as a home for Argent, the Silver Dragon, and his lair. A messenger delivers food and supplies every two weeks.

Dragon
ARGENT THE
SILVER DRAGON

Argent has been guarding the Silver Key since the wizards of the north first made it, many years ago.

DRAGON MASTER

Jean Arcand

POWER COLOR

SIZE

LENGTH: 36 feet

WEIGHT: 11,300 pounds

- Argent can blast his enemies with his silver shine.

- When opponents attack, Argent can use his shiny wings to reflect their attack right back at them.

Training Tip

The only way for Argent to practice reflecting attacks is if he has another dragon to practice with. Jean may call on her new friends for help with practicing this power — although Argent is already really great at it!

Along with the Silver Key, Argent guards all of King Leon's silver treasure.

-Griffith

Dragon Master
DARMA LI

HOME

Darma has always lived on the Island of Suvarna.

STRENGTHS

Darma is very in tune with the world around him. He may have learned some of these skills from the monks who raised him. He can sense what might happen in the near future. Because of his strong connection to the world around him, he always believes that everything will turn out all right. This keeps him calm in dangerous situations. He can also feel the energy of portals and magical objects and places.

Is Darma Magic?

Drake and Rori wondered this when they met Darma. Other Dragon Masters are not able to feel magical energy or sense what is about to happen in the future. Griffith thought Darma might be a young wizard, but Darma is not a wizard. He learned these skills in the temple where he was raised.

Darma lost his parents when he was a baby. He was raised in a temple by the monks who live there. A monk named Budi became his adopted father.

DRAGON

Hema the Gold Dragon

THE ISLAND OF SUVARNA

Glory Peak

Ash Mountains

Cloud Mountains

Blue Fire Volcanoes

Great Sea

This island is very, very far from Bracken. It is even farther than the kingdom of Emperor Song. Suvarna is divided up into twelve kingdoms. Darma lives in the land ruled by King Wisnu the Brave.

It is very hot in Suvarna. The land is covered with green plants and colorful flowers. It is one of the few places in the world where you can find the Rainbow Tree — a tree with bark that grows in different-colored stripes, like a rainbow.

The people there are great builders. They build palaces and temples that touch the sky.

Dragons are more common in Suvarna than in some other places. You can find Water Dragons there, and Flower Dragons connected to nature. But Hema the Gold Dragon is the greatest dragon on the island.

Dragon
HEMA THE
GOLD DRAGON

Hema has been guarding the Gold Key since the wizards of the south first made it, many years ago.

DRAGON MASTER

Darma Li

POWER COLOR

SIZE

LENGTH: 34 feet

WEIGHT: 12,400 pounds

- Hema can shoot beams of golden energy from her mouth. Those beams can blast her opponents, or wrap around them as though with a rope.

- She can change into any animal form she wants to.

Training Tip

Be careful not to ask Hema to transform into anything too small. Darma once asked Hema to turn into a flea, and then spent three hours trying to find her.

I would love to figure out how Hema's powers work. It is amazing that she can transform from a big dragon into a tiny mouse.

-Griffith

URI AND ZELDA

HOME

Uri and Zelda have always lived on the Dragon Islands.

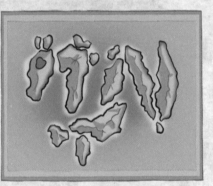

STRENGTHS

Uri and Zelda have one of the most difficult jobs a Dragon Master can have. They must work with the Naga to help keep the world safe! These twins are able to tap into the power of the Naga. It makes them very strong. Using the Naga's powers, they can float in the air, and even launch energy attacks at anyone who threatens the Naga.

Uri and Zelda's mother, Chandra, and her twin brother, Ravi, were also Dragon Masters for the Naga.

The Twin Connection

The Dragon Stone chooses twins for the Naga every time, and they all come from the same family. Only the Naga has two Dragon Masters, probably because more than one is needed to control the massive dragon.

DRAGON

The Naga, also known as the Earthquake Dragon

Because Uri and Zelda can tap into the Naga's powers, that means they are Dragon Mages. This is unusual — most Dragon Masters do not become Dragon Mages until they are adults. Their strong minds — and the strong powers of the Naga — might explain why this has happened so fast.

-Griffith

THE TEMPLE OF THE NAGA

Uri and Zelda connect with the Naga in this temple, which is located in the Dragon Islands.

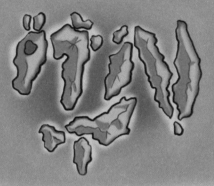

Wizards built this temple on the spot where the two keys sent the Naga into the center of the earth. The wizards added a layer of Dragon Stone under the floor to help the Dragon Masters' minds reach the Naga deep in the earth. They created a door that opens to reveal the Naga's eye. The Naga's Dragon Masters can open the door. But it can also be opened using the Silver Key and the Gold Key. The keys fit inside the eyes of the dragon statue on top of the door. Once the door is opened, the Dragon Masters must summon the Naga with a chant.

Anyone who uses the keys to open the door can control the Naga's Dragon Masters. And whoever controls them can control the Naga!

- The Naga can cause earthquakes simply by turning his eye to a place. He uses the power of his mind to cause an earthquake there.

- The Naga can shoot powerful energy blasts from his eyes.

The Naga may be the most powerful dragon in the world.

-Griffith

POWER COLOR

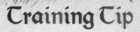Uri and Zelda's main job is to keep the Naga calm and safe. When they train, they are learning how to channel the Naga's power and use it themselves to defend the temple.

SIZE

This dragon is so large that there is no way to measure him!

BREEN HANIGAN

HOME

Breen lives in Inis Banba. She often visits her dragon, Fallyn, in the secret fairy world there.

STRENGTHS

Breen has a good sense of humor. And she is very clever. She also loves riddles and playing games, which is helpful when dealing with the fairy world.

A Friendly Monster

Blorp is a scary-looking ogre who is a friend of Breen's. Blorp is basically a good creature, but stay away from him when he's hungry!

Breen is the youngest of seven sisters. Her mother, Ina, is also the youngest of seven sisters, and is known for baking delicious cakes. Her father, Conall, is a beekeeper.

DRAGON

Fallyn the Spring Dragon

ÍNIS BANBA

Inis Banba is an island to the west of Albion. It is sometimes called the Green Island because of the rich green countryside there. Now we know that the land is so green because of Fallyn the Spring Dragon.

Vast Sea

Inis Sea

Ancient Ocean

It is a good thing that Drake had Breen as his guide when he went there!

-Griffith

The Fairy World of Inis Banba

Fallyn lives underneath the green hills — in a secret fairy world. The fairy world looks almost like the world above it, but it is different. The sky is pink instead of blue. Colors look brighter. And all kinds of tricky magical fairy creatures live there, such as redcaps, pookas, and Hinky Pink.

The entrance to this world is a small hill known as the fairy mound. A wizard can usually get into the mound using magic. Breen's connection to her dragon means she can enter whenever she likes. And sometimes, fairies open up the door from the inside and human travelers get sucked in. Legends warn that if you enter the fairy world, you may never get out.

Hinky Pink

Travelers get lost in Hinky Pink's magical fog.

Pooka

The Pooka can take any form, but likes being a horse the best.

Dragon
FALLYN THE
SPRING DRAGON

Fallyn may look like a cute dragon, but her power to make things grow is amazing!

DRAGON MASTER

Breen Hanigan

Legend says that Fallyn's Dragon Master must be a seventh daughter of a seventh daughter.

-Griffith

POWERS

- Fallyn can make plants of all kinds grow anywhere almost instantly.

- After winter is over, Fallyn brings spring to the land of Inis Banba.

POWER COLOR

SIZE

LENGTH: 23 feet

WEIGHT: 3,000 pounds

Training Tip

Breen is confident that Fallyn knows what she is doing. She prefers to sing songs and play games with Fallyn instead of training her.

NATURE DRAGONS

Some dragons are strongly connected to the seasons of nature in the land where they live.

Spring Dragons and Rainbow Dragons are Nature Dragons. You can usually find Spring Dragons in places that have a lot of plants and flowers. And Rainbow Dragons are very important to places that don't get enough water.

Other Nature Dragons include a Tree Dragon in the Western Lands that changes the color of the leaves in the forest, and a Wind Dragon that brings winds to the high mountains of Itzel. And in the Himala Mountains, there are legends of a Winter Dragon that brings the cold and snow.

These are just a few of the Nature Dragons that live all over the world. There are probably many more types to discover!

Not all Nature Dragons have epic powers. Some Flower Dragons only reach six inches in height. They make flowers sprout wherever they walk.

-Griffith

Dragon Mage
EKO IHARA

HOME

Eko grew up in the land of Hayan in the Far East. She lived in Bracken for a few years when she became Neru's Dragon Master. Then she moved to an island in the Southern Ocean.

STRENGTHS

Because Eko has a strong will, she does not always like following the rules. She is a Dragon Mage, so she can harness Neru's purple energy. She can use it like a whip to wrap around something. And she once used Neru's powers to stop Worm from transporting.

Eko was the first Dragon Master trained by Griffith of the Green Fields. The Dragon Stone chose her after King Roland got his first dragon — Neru, a Thunder Dragon.

Eko loved Neru, and she loved being a Dragon Master. But she never liked following Griffith's or King Roland's rules. And when the king began searching for more dragons to bring to the castle, she thought he was wrong. She thought all dragons should be free — even though she had a strong connection to Neru.

Eko left the castle and took Neru with her. She did not return until years later, when she attacked Bracken and tried to free all the dragons. She could not see how she was hurting the dragons or their Dragon Masters. She is often only able to see one point of view — her own.

DRAGON

Neru the Thunder Dragon

Rori reminds me of Eko, when Eko was the same age...

-Griffith

NERU THE THUNDER DRAGON

When you hear a loud boom in the sky, it may be thunder — or it may be Neru!

POWER COLOR

POWERS

- Neru can create a purple shield that protects him from attacks.

- His huge thunder booms shake the earth and knock dragons out of the sky.

- He can make portals that allow him to travel to faraway places.

A portal is a magical doorway from one place to another.

-Griffith

DRAGON MASTER

Eko Ihara

SIZE

LENGTH: 27 feet

WEIGHT: 4,800 pounds

Training Tip

If you are training a Thunder Dragon, make sure you have a very strong connection before you try creating portals. If the portal isn't done right, you could end up someplace you don't expect — and it might not be easy to get back!

BECOMING A DRAGON MAGE

When a Dragon Master is first chosen by the Dragon Stone, he or she begins learning how to work with their dragon. The more they train together, the stronger their connection becomes.

After several years of training, a connection between a Dragon Master and dragon can become very strong. The Dragon Master can learn how to tap into the powers of their dragon and use them as their own. When this happens, a Dragon Master becomes a Dragon Mage.

Eko, a former student of Griffith of the Green Fields, is now a Dragon Mage. She can harness the purple energy of her Thunder Dragon, Neru. Uri and Zelda, the Dragon Masters of the Naga, also appear to be Dragon Mages.

Dragon Mages will never be able to copy the full powers of their dragons. Eko cannot make thunder blasts the way that Neru can. But she can harness Neru's energy and turn it into power blasts, force fields, and energy leashes.

Not all Dragon Masters become Dragon Mages. But the best Dragon Masters will reach this level one day!

HEAR YE! HEAR YE!
From the Royal Quill of King Roland

I am King Roland the Bold of the Kingdom of Bracken. Griffith told me that he and Tracey of the West were putting together a book about dragons. I want to make sure they don't leave out the most important part: why Bracken needs dragons.

Bracken is a beautiful kingdom! A wide river runs through our land. Our fields grow the best crops. Everyone in Albion says we grow the best onions!

Because we are so great, other kingdoms are jealous of us. They have attacked us in the past so that they could take over our wonderful land and kick us out. But now nobody will attack us, because we have DRAGONS! Word has spread far and wide about our awesome dragons who will save the kingdom when we need them to. So, dragons — and their Dragon Masters — keep Bracken safe.

Besides being very powerful, my dragons put on a great show! They really impressed Queen Rose when I brought them to Arkwood, before the queen and I got married. And they did some awesome tricks at our wedding parade! The big brown one that looks like a worm made flowers dance in the air. Queen Rose really liked that.

So, in conclusion, Bracken's dragons are THE BEST! That is all.

King Roland

Worm's dancing flowers were the hit of the parade!
-Griffith

DARK FORCES AFOOT

I was very excited when King Roland began bringing dragons to Bracken. It gave me a chance to study them up close. And of course, I enjoyed meeting each new Dragon Master.

But one problem with having so many dragons in one place is that someone with an evil heart could try to steal them and use them to create a powerful army. A person with that kind of army could rule the world!

For this reason, Dragon Masters need to know about all the dark forces out there. Future Dragon Masters must learn how to combat these forces and defend peace.

There are greedy kings, dark wizards, and even magical creatures to worry about . . .

-Griffith

Vasty the Ice Giant

Long ago, Ice Giants ruled the Far North Lands. Then the humans drove them out. One Ice Giant named Vasty became trapped in a tomb of ice. When he awoke, he froze the castle of King Lars and everyone in it! He's not giant anymore, though, thanks to Vulcan. The Fire Dragon's powers shrank Vasty into a tiny creature.

Kwaku the Spider

Kwaku is a giant spider that lives in the Kingdom of Ifri. The people of Ifri tell stories about Kwaku. They say he likes to play tricks. He is not always dangerous. But if you see this giant spider, stay away!

The Redcaps

These magical little men march around the fairy world beneath Inis Banba. They may look cute, but if they find a human to play with, they will try to get that person to march behind them forever!

Wizard

MALDRED OF THE RED HILLS

MAGIC LEVEL

It has never been tested, but his level is at least a 71.

COLOR OF MAGIC

POWERS

Maldred can do many things with his dark powers. He can freeze or zap his opponents with a blast of red energy. He can cast spells to make them obey him. His red magic bubbles can trap opponents. A sprinkle of his red magic dust can transport people or objects a short distance. He creates magical orbs that he can send to a place far away. And once, he created a red Dragon Stone that he used to control a dragon!

Maldred grew up in the harsh lands of Redbern. Life is not easy there. It is burning hot in the daytime and freezing cold at night.

When Maldred discovered that he could do magic, he did not go to the Castle of the Wizards. Nobody in his land knew about wizards, so they were afraid of him and his powers. He was sent away from his village, with nowhere to go.

In order to survive on his own, Maldred was forced to use his magic. For this reason, his magic became very strong. But because he had no teachers, there was nobody to guide him or to warn him about the dangerous pull of dark magic.

Today, he is one of the most powerful wizards the world has ever seen.

Red Alert

A wizard's magical energy can be any color. But wizards who use dark magic, like Maldred, always seem to have red energy.

MALDRED'S WORKSHOP

Maldred's workshop is located in a magical dimension. Drake, Rori, and Darma found it using the energy from a portal.

Besides being hidden in a magical dimension, it seems to be like any other wizard's workshop. Maldred has shelves of books, and potions, and ingredients for potions.

Dark Spells
Maldred's books are mostly spells for dark magic.

Magic Eye
Maldred uses this to hypnotize anyone who stands in front of it.

The workshop is in a large tower with a spiral staircase.

The walls at the top of the tower have a strange pattern of wizard faces on them.

Journals

He keeps a record of all of his magical battles.

Red Magic

This potion is the main ingredient in Maldred's red magical orbs.

THE WORLD OF THE DRAGON MASTERS

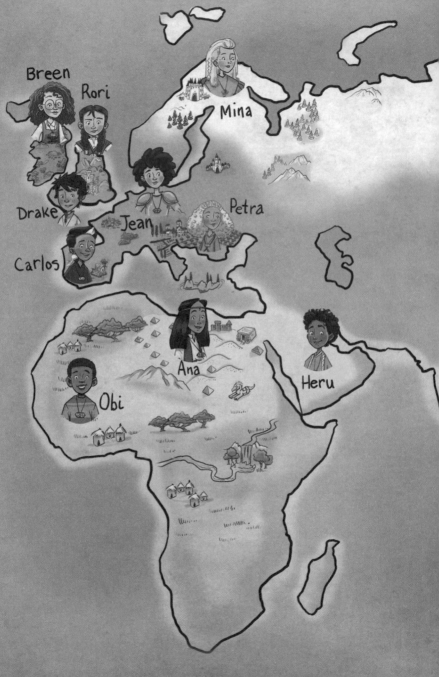

Never Forget!

If you have read this entire book, you are on your way to becoming a better Dragon Master. Maybe one day you will even be a Dragon Mage!

I will leave you with one last bit of advice. This is something I tell all of my Dragon Masters. To be a good Dragon Master, remember these three things:

1. <u>Kindness</u>: Be kind to your dragon, your fellow Dragon Masters, and everyone you meet in your travels.

2. <u>Curiosity</u>: Keep your eyes and your mind open so that you learn new things from the places you go and the people you meet.

3. <u>Teamwork</u>: When Dragon Masters work together, great things can happen!

Yours in magic,

Griffith of the Green Fields

TRACEY OF THE WEST lives in a cottage in the misty mountains. She wishes she had been a Dragon Master, but since she wasn't chosen by the Dragon Stone, she writes about dragons instead.

MATT LOVERIDGE is one of King Roland's royal illustrators. The king says, "His dragon drawings are the BEST!" He lives in the Rocky Mountains of the Far, Far, West with his wife and five children. His kids all hope to be Dragon Masters someday.

10 9 8 7 6   21 22 23

Printed in China   62
First edition, December 2019
Illustrated by Matt Loveridge
Edited by Katie Carella
Book design by Sarah Dvojack